Walt Disney's

MOTHER GOOSE

Illustrations by

THE WALT DISNEY STUDIO

A GOLDEN BOOK • NEW YORK

Western Publishing Company, Inc., Racine, Wisconsin 53404

THE OLD WOMAN
WHO LIVED IN A SHOE

There was an old woman who lived in a shoe;
She had so many children she didn't know what to do.
She gave them some broth without any bread;
She whipped them all soundly and sent them to bed.

DING, DONG, BELL

Ding, dong, bell,
Pussy's in the well!
Who put her in?
Little Tommy Lin.
Who pulled her out?
Big Johnny Stout.
What a naughty boy was that
To try to drown poor pussy cat,
Who never did him any harm,
But killed the mice in his father's barn.

PAT-A-CAKE

Pat-a-cake, pat-a-cake,
    Baker's man.
Bake me a cake,
    As fast as you can.
Pat it and prick it
    And mark it with B.
Put it in the oven
    For Baby and me.

A DILLAR, A DOLLAR

A dillar, a dollar,
A ten o'clock scholar,
What makes you come so soon?
You used to come at ten o'clock,
And now you come at noon.

HEY DIDDLE, DIDDLE

Hey diddle, diddle, the cat and the fiddle,
The cow jumped over the moon;
The little dog laughed to see such sport,
And the dish ran away with the spoon.

BYE, BABY BUNTING

Bye, baby bunting,
Daddy's gone a-hunting,
To get a little rabbit's skin
To wrap the baby bunting in.

LITTLE TOMMY TITTLEMOUSE

Little Tommy Tittlemouse
Lived in a little house;
He caught fishes
In other men's ditches.

THE QUEEN
OF HEARTS

The Queen of Hearts,
She made some tarts
All on a summer's day.
The Knave of Hearts,
He stole the tarts
And with them ran away.

The King of Hearts
Called for the tarts
And beat the Knave full sore.
The Knave of Hearts
Brought back the tarts
And vowed he'd steal no more.

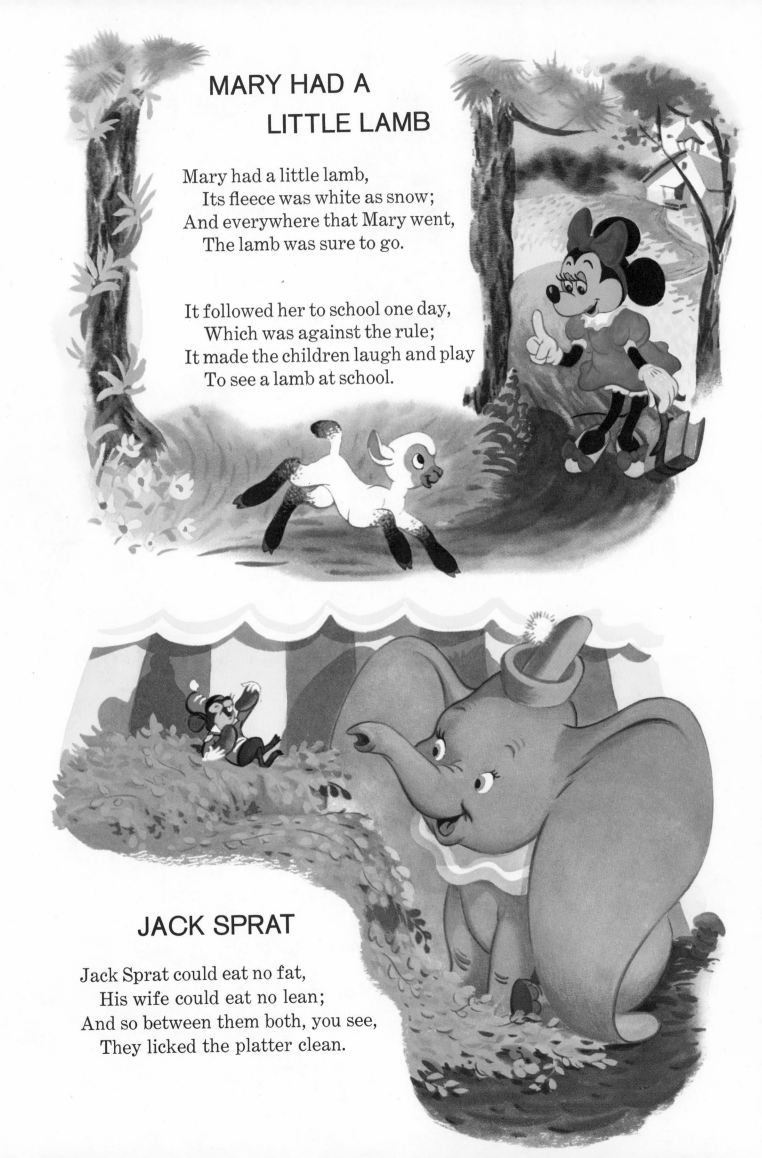

MARY HAD A
LITTLE LAMB

Mary had a little lamb,
Its fleece was white as snow;
And everywhere that Mary went,
The lamb was sure to go.

It followed her to school one day,
Which was against the rule;
It made the children laugh and play
To see a lamb at school.

JACK SPRAT

Jack Sprat could eat no fat,
His wife could eat no lean;
And so between them both, you see,
They licked the platter clean.

CROSS PATCH

Cross patch,
Draw the latch,
Sit by the fire and spin;
Take a cup
And drink it up,
And call your neighbors in.

LITTLE BOY BLUE

Little Boy Blue, come, blow your horn;
The sheep's in the meadow, the cow's in the corn.
Where's the boy that looks after the sheep?
He's under the haystack, fast asleep.

THE JOLLY MILLER

There was a jolly miller once,
Lived on the river Dee;
He worked and sang from morn till night,
No lark more blithe than he.

And this the burden of his song
Forever used to be—
"I care for nobody, no! not I,
If nobody cares for me."

DOCTOR FOSTER

Doctor Foster went to Gloucester
In a shower of rain;
He stepped in a puddle up to his middle
And never went there again.

GEORGIE PORGIE

Georgie Porgie, pudding and pie,
Kissed the girls and made them cry.
When the boys came out to play,
Georgie Porgie ran away.

LITTLE JACK HORNER

Little Jack Horner sat in a corner
Eating a Christmas pie;
He put in his thumb, and pulled out a plum
And said, "What a good boy am I!"

THREE WISE MEN
OF GOTHAM

Three wise men of Gotham
Went to sea in a bowl.
If the bowl had been stronger,
My song would have been longer.

RIDE A COCKHORSE

Ride a cockhorse to Banbury Cross
To see a fine lady upon a white horse.
Rings on her fingers, and bells on her toes,
She shall have music wherever she goes.

PETER, PETER, PUMPKIN EATER

Peter, Peter, pumpkin eater,
Had a wife and couldn't keep her;
He put her in a pumpkin shell
And there he kept her very well.

THIS LITTLE PIG

This little pig went to market,
This little pig stayed at home,
This little pig had roast beef,
This little pig had none,
And this little pig cried, "Wee-wee-wee,"
All the way home.

THIS IS THE WAY
THE LADIES RIDE

This is the way the ladies ride:
Tri, tre, tre, tree! Tri, tre, tre, tree!

This is the way the gentlemen ride:
Gallop-a-trot! Gallop-a-trot!

This is the way the farmers ride:
Hobbledy-hoy! Hobbledy-hoy!

JACK AND JILL

Jack and Jill went up the hill
   To fetch a pail of water.
Jack fell down and broke his crown,
   And Jill came tumbling after.

Then up Jack got, and home did trot
   As fast as he could caper,
Went to bed and plastered his head
   With vinegar and brown paper.

ROCK-A-BYE, BABY

Rock-a-bye, baby, on the tree top!
When the wind blows, the cradle will rock;
When the bough breaks, the cradle will fall;
Down will come baby, cradle and all.

HICKETY, PICKETY

Hickety, pickety, my black hen,
She lays eggs for gentlemen;
Gentlemen come every day
To see what my black hen doth lay.
Sometimes nine and sometimes ten,
Hickety, pickety, my black hen.

RUB A DUB DUB

Rub a dub dub,
Three men in a tub,
And who do you think they be?
The butcher, the baker,
The candlestick maker;
Turn 'em out, knaves all three!

LITTLE TOMMY TUCKER

Little Tommy Tucker
Sings for his supper.
What shall he eat?
White bread and butter.

How shall he cut it
Without e'er a knife?
How shall he marry
Without e'er a wife?

CURLY LOCKS

Curly Locks, Curly Locks, wilt thou be mine?
Thou shalt not wash dishes, nor yet feed the swine,
But sit on a cushion and sew a fine seam,
And feed upon strawberries, sugar and cream.

LITTLE MISS MUFFET

Little Miss Muffet
Sat on a tuffet,
Eating her curds and whey;
There came a big spider
Who sat down beside her
And frightened Miss Muffet away.

HICKORY, DICKORY, DOCK

Hickory, dickory, dock,
The mouse ran up the clock.
The clock struck one,
And down he run;
Hickory, dickory, dock.

HANDY PANDY

Handy Pandy,
   Jack-a-dandy,
Loved plum cake
   and sugar candy;
He bought some
   at a grocer's shop,
And out he came,
   hop, hop, hop.

HUMPTY DUMPTY

Humpty Dumpty
   sat on a wall,
Humpty Dumpty
   had a great fall;
All the King's horses
   and all the King's men
Couldn't put Humpty Dumpty
   together again.

MISTRESS MARY

Mistress Mary, quite contrary,
How does your garden grow?
With silver bells and cockle shells
And pretty maids all in a row.

BAA, BAA, BLACK SHEEP

Baa, baa, black sheep, have you any wool?
Yes, sir, yes, sir, three bags full;
One for my master, one for my dame,
And one for the little boy who lives down the lane.

SING A SONG OF SIXPENCE

Sing a song of sixpence, a pocket full of rye,
Four and twenty blackbirds, baked in a pie;
When the pie was opened, the birds began to sing;
Wasn't that a dainty dish to set before the king?

The king was in his counting-house, counting out his money;
The queen was in the parlor, eating bread and honey;
The maid was in the garden, hanging out the clothes;
There came a little blackbird, and snipped off her nose.

THERE WAS AN OLD WOMAN

There was an old woman tossed up in a basket,
    Seventeen times as high as the moon;
And where she was going, I couldn't but ask it,
    For under her arm she carried a broom.

"Old woman, old woman, old woman," said I,
    "Whither, oh whither, oh whither so high?"
"To sweep the cobwebs out of the sky!"
    "Shall I go with you?" "Yes, by and by."

WEE WILLIE WINKIE

Wee Willie Winkie runs through the town,
Upstairs and downstairs, in his nightgown;
Rapping at the window, crying through the lock,
"Are the children all in bed, for now it's eight o'clock?"

Walt Disney's
Mickey Mouse
The KITTEN-SITTERS

A GOLDEN BOOK • NEW YORK
Western Publishing Company, Inc., Racine, Wisconsin 53404

"Guess what!" said Mickey Mouse to his nephews, Morty and Ferdie. "We're going to be kitten-sitters. Minnie is going to leave Figaro the kitten with us tonight while she visits her Cousin Millie."

At that moment, there was a wild clucking and flapping and crowing from next door. Pluto the pup came racing across the lawn, with a big, angry rooster close behind him.

Pluto hid under the porch while Mickey shooed the rooster back to his own yard.

"Pluto!" scolded Minnie. "Chasing chickens again! Aren't you ashamed?"

Pluto *was* a bit ashamed, but only because he had let the rooster bully him. Creeping out from under the porch, he wagged his tail and sheepishly tried to grin.

"I think it's a good thing Figaro is going to stay with you," said Minnie to Mickey. "Figaro is a little gentleman. He can teach Pluto how to behave."

With that, Minnie handed her kitten to Mickey. Then she got into her car and drove away.

Minnie was scarcely out of sight, when Figaro jumped out of Mickey's arms and scampered into the house. In the kitchen, he saw a pitcher of cream that Mickey had forgotten to put away.

One short jump up to a chair seat, followed by a second jump to the tabletop, brought Figaro right to the cream. The pitcher wobbled, then tipped over. Cream spilled and ran off the table and onto the floor.

Pluto growled a warning growl as Figaro lapped up the delicious cream.

"Take it easy, Pluto," said Mickey, wiping up the spilled cream. "Figaro is our guest."

When Figaro heard that, he wrinkled his nose at Pluto and stuck out his little pink tongue.

Then he romped through the ashes in the fireplace and left sooty footprints on the carpet.

"Figaro's a very *messy* little guest," said Mickey's nephew Morty as he got out the vacuum cleaner.

At dinner time, Pluto ate his dog food, the way a good dog should. But no matter how Mickey and the boys coaxed, Figaro wouldn't touch the special kitty food Minnie had left for him. He did, at last, nibble some imported sardines.

"He's a *fussy* little guest," said Ferdie.

At bedtime, Pluto curled up in his basket without any complaint.

Did Figaro curl up on the fine, soft cushion Minnie had brought for him? He did not!

Instead, he got into bed with Morty and nipped at his toes. Then he got into bed with Ferdie and tickled both of his ears. Finally, he bounced off to the kitchen, and the house became very still.

"Uncle Mickey," called Morty, "did you remember to close the kitchen window?"

"Oh, no!" cried Mickey. He jumped out of bed and ran to the kitchen.

The kitchen window was open, and Figaro the kitten was nowhere to be seen!

Mickey and the boys went through the house. They looked under every chair and behind every door.
"Figaro!" they called.

They went out into the yard. They looked under every
bush and behind every tree.
No Figaro.

"He's really run away," Mickey decided at last. Morty and Ferdie followed Mickey back to the house, where Mickey put his coat on over his pajamas. "You two stay here," he told the boys. "Pluto and I will find Figaro. Leave the porch light on for us."

Pluto didn't wag his tail, and he didn't even try to grin as he got out of his cozy basket. But off he went to help Mickey in the search.

They went to Minnie's house first, but Figaro hadn't gone back home.

Then they went to the park down the street. "Have you seen a little black and white kitten?" Mickey asked the policeman at the gate.

"I certainly have!" answered the policeman. "He was by the pond, teasing the ducks!"

Mickey and Pluto hurried to the pond.

Figaro wasn't there. He had been there, though. He had left behind some small, muddy footprints and several large, excited ducks.

Mickey and Pluto followed the trail of footprints to Main Street, where they met a crew of firemen.

"I'm looking for a black and white kitten," said Mickey to the firemen.

"Is that so?" said one of the firemen. "We just rescued a black and white kitten. He had climbed a telephone pole and couldn't get down again. He ran through that alley."

In the alley, a dairy truck driver was busily cleaning up broken eggs in his truck.

"Have you seen a kitten?" asked Mickey.

"Have I!" said the driver. "He jumped into my truck and knocked over dozens of eggs!"

Mickey groaned as he paid for the smashed eggs.

When Mickey and Pluto finally trudged home, it was dawn. They had searched the whole town. They had even been to the police station, but they had not found Figaro.

"What will Aunt Minnie say?" asked the boys.

"I hate to think what Aunt Minnie will say," answered poor Mickey.

Before long, Minnie drove up. Mickey and the boys looked worried as they went out to meet her.

"Where is Figaro?" asked Minnie.

No one answered.

"Something has happened to him!" Minnie was upset, and she was angry. "Can't I trust you to watch *just one* sweet little kitten for me?"

Just then there was a loud clucking and squawking from the yard next door. At least a dozen frantic hens came flapping over the fence.

Close behind the hens came the big, angry rooster. Close behind the rooster came Figaro the kitten. Figaro's fur was rumpled, and he carried a long tail feather between his clenched teeth.

"There's your sweet little kitten!" said Mickey.

"Figaro!" cried Minnie, not believing her eyes.

At the sound of her voice, Figaro skidded to a sudden stop. He sat down and mewed a gentle kitten mew. He tried quickly to smooth his dusty fur with his little pink tongue.

"He ran away last night," explained Mickey. "He teased the ducks in the park and broke the eggs in the dairy truck and—"

"And now he's chasing chickens!" finished Minnie.

"I hoped he'd teach Pluto some manners," Minnie went on. "Instead, Pluto has been teaching him to do those naughty things. Teasing ducks! Chasing chickens! The very idea! I'll *never* leave him here again."

"It wasn't Pluto's fault!" protested Morty.

"He didn't do anything bad," added Ferdie. "He stayed up all night, trying to find Figaro."

But Minnie wouldn't listen. She picked up Figaro, got into her car, and drove quickly away.

"Don't worry, boys," said Mickey. "We'll tell her the whole story later, when she's not so upset."

"Please don't tell her too soon," begged Morty. "As long as Aunt Minnie thinks Pluto is a naughty dog, we won't have to kitten-sit with Figaro."

Mickey smiled. "Maybe we *should* wait a little while. We could all use some peace and quiet.

"I did learn one thing," yawned Mickey as he stretched out beside Pluto under a shady tree. "There's not much sitting in kitten-sitting."

WALT DISNEY'S

Winnie·the·Pooh
The Unbouncing of Tigger

WALT DISNEY'S

Winnie·the·Pooh
The Unbouncing of Tigger

A Story by A. A. MILNE

A GOLDEN BOOK • NEW YORK
Western Publishing Company, Inc., Racine, Wisconsin 53404

One day, Piglet was sitting outside Pooh's front door listening to Rabbit, and Pooh was sitting right beside him.

It was a drowsy summer afternoon, and the Forest was full of gentle sounds, which all seemed to be saying to Pooh, "Don't listen to Rabbit, listen to me."

"In fact," said Rabbit, coming to the end of it at last, "Tigger's getting so Bouncy nowadays that it's time we taught him a lesson. Don't you think so, Piglet?"

Piglet said that Tigger *was* very Bouncy, and that if they could think of a way of unbouncing him, it would be a Very Good Idea.

"Well, I've got an idea," said Rabbit, "and here it is. We take Tigger for a long explore, somewhere he's never been, and we lose him there, and next morning we find him again, and—mark my words—he'll be a different Tigger altogether."

"Why?" said Pooh.

"Because he'll be a Humble Tigger, a Sad Tigger, an Oh-Rabbit-I-*am*-glad-to-see-you Tigger. That's why. If we can make Tigger feel Small and Sad just for five minutes, it will be a good deed."

So it was arranged that they should start next morning.

The next day was quite a different day. Instead of being hot and sunny, it was cold and misty.

At first Pooh and Rabbit and Piglet walked together, and Tigger ran round them in circles; and then, when the path got narrower, Rabbit, Piglet, and Pooh plodded one after another, and Tigger ran round them in oblongs; and by-and-by, when the gorse got very prickly on each side of the path, Tigger ran up and down in front of them; and sometimes he bounced into Rabbit and sometimes he didn't.

And as they got higher, the mist got thicker, so that Tigger kept disappearing, and then when you thought he wasn't there, there he was again, saying, "I say, come on," and before you could say anything, there he wasn't.

Rabbit turned around and nudged Piglet.

"The next time," he said. "Tell Pooh."

"The next time," said Piglet to Pooh.

"The next what?" said Pooh to Piglet.

Tigger appeared suddenly, bounced into Rabbit, and disappeared again.

"Now!" said Rabbit.

Rabbit jumped into a hollow by the side of the path, and Pooh and Piglet jumped after him. They crouched in the bracken, listening.

The Forest was very silent when you stopped and listened to it.

They could see nothing and hear nothing.

"H'sh!" said Rabbit.

"I am," said Pooh.

There was a pattering noise . . . then silence again.

"Hallo!" said Tigger, and he sounded so close suddenly that Piglet would have jumped if Pooh hadn't accidentally been sitting on most of him.

"Where are you?" called Tigger.

Rabbit nudged Pooh, and Pooh looked about for Piglet to nudge but couldn't find him, and Piglet went on breathing wet bracken as quietly as he could and felt very brave and excited.

"That's funny," said Tigger.

There was a moment's silence, and then they heard him pattering off again. For a little longer they waited, until the Forest had become so still that it almost frightened them.

Then Rabbit got up and stretched himself.

"Well?" Rabbit whispered proudly. "There we are! Just as I said."

"I've been thinking," said Pooh, "and I think—"

"No," said Rabbit. "Don't. Run. Come on." And they all hurried off, Rabbit leading the way.

"Now," said Rabbit, after they had gone a little way, "we can talk. What were you going to say, Pooh?"

"Nothing much. Why are we going along here?"

"Because it's the way home."

"Oh!" said Pooh.

"Come on," said Rabbit. "I know it's this way."

"Here we are," said Rabbit ten minutes later. "No, we're not...."

"It's a funny thing," said Rabbit another ten minutes later, "how everything looks the same in a mist. Have you noticed it, Pooh?"

Pooh said that he had.

"Lucky we know the Forest so well, or we might get lost," said Rabbit half an hour later, and he gave the careless laugh that you give when you know the Forest so well that you can't get lost.

Piglet sidled up to Pooh from behind. "Pooh!"

"Yes, Piglet?"

"Nothing," said Piglet, taking Pooh's paw. "I just wanted to be sure of you."

When Tigger had finished waiting for the others to catch him up, and they hadn't, and when he had got tired of having nobody to say "I say, come on" to, he thought he would go home. So he trotted back; and the first thing Kanga said when she saw him was "Now, here comes a good Tigger. You're just in time for your Strengthening Syrup," and she poured it out for him.

And it was just as they were finishing dinner that Christopher Robin put his head in at the door.

"Where's Pooh?" he asked.

"Tigger dear, where's Pooh?" said Kanga. Tigger explained what had happened at the same time that Roo was explaining and Kanga was telling them not both to talk at once, so it was some time before Christopher Robin guessed that Pooh and Piglet and Rabbit were all lost in the mist of the Forest.

"It's a funny thing about Tiggers," whispered Tigger
to Roo, "how Tiggers *never* get lost."

"Why don't they, Tigger?"

"They just don't," explained Tigger. "That's how it is."

"Well," said Christopher Robin, "we shall have to go
and find them, that's all. Come on, Tigger."

"I shall have to go and find them," explained
Tigger to Roo. . . .

Pooh, Rabbit, and Piglet were having a rest in a small sandpit in the Forest. Pooh was getting rather tired of that sandpit, and he suspected it of following them about.

"The fact is," said Rabbit, "we've missed our way somehow."

"How would it be," said Pooh slowly, "if, as soon as we're out of sight of this Pit, we try to find it again?"

"What's the good of that?" asked Rabbit.

"Well," said Pooh, "we keep looking for Home and not finding it, so I thought that if we looked for this

Pit, we'd be sure not to find it, which would be a Good Thing, because then we might find something that we *weren't* looking for, which might be exactly what we *were* looking for, really."

"I don't see much sense in that," said Rabbit. "If I walked away from this Pit, and then walked back to it, of *course* I should find it."

"Well, I thought perhaps you wouldn't," said Pooh. "I just thought."

"Try," said Piglet suddenly. "We'll wait here for you."

Rabbit gave a laugh to show how silly Piglet was and walked into the mist. After he had gone a hundred yards, he turned and walked back again . . . and after Pooh and Piglet had waited twenty minutes for him, Pooh got up.

"I just thought," said Pooh. "Now, then, Piglet, let's go home."

"But, Pooh," cried Piglet, all excited, "do you know the way?"

"No," said Pooh. "But, you see, there are twelve pots of honey in my cupboard, and they've been calling to me for hours.

"I couldn't hear them properly before," he continued, "because Rabbit *would* talk, but if nobody says anything except those twelve pots, I *think*, Piglet, I shall know where they're calling from. Come on."

They walked off together; and for a long time Piglet said nothing, so as not to interrupt the pots; and then suddenly he made a squeaky noise . . . and an *oo*-noise . . . because now he began to know where he was; but he still didn't dare to say so out loud, in case he wasn't.

And just when he was getting so sure of himself that it didn't matter whether the pots went on calling or not, there was a shout from in front of them, and out of the mist came Christopher Robin.

"Oh, there you are," said Christopher Robin carelessly, trying to pretend that he hadn't been Anxious.

"Here we are," said Pooh.

"Where's Rabbit?"

"I don't know," said Pooh.

"Oh—well, I expect Tigger will find him. He's sort of looking for you all."

"Well," said Pooh, "I've got to go home for something, and so has Piglet, because we haven't had it yet, and—"

"I'll come and watch you," said Christopher Robin.

So he went home with Pooh, and he watched him for quite a long time . . .

. . . and all the time he was watching, Tigger was tearing round the Forest making loud yapping noises for Rabbit.

And at last a very Small and Sorry Rabbit heard him. And the Small and Sorry Rabbit rushed through the mist at the noise.

And the noise suddenly turned into Tigger; a Friendly Tigger, a Grand Tigger, a Large and Helpful Tigger, a Tigger who bounced, if he bounced at all, in just the beautiful way a Tigger ought to bounce.

"Oh, Tigger, I *am* glad to see you," cried Rabbit.